Little People, BIG DREAMS®

MOTHER TERESA

Written by
Maria Isabel Sánchez Vegara

Illustrated by
Natascha Rosenberg

Frances Lincoln
Children's Books

Once, there was a little Albanian girl who was always willing to give a helping hand. Her name was Agnes, and she lived in Skopje, with her parents and two siblings.

Agnes was raised to love God and love others above all else. Little did she know that in the future she would be known as Saint Teresa of Calcutta...

One day, a new priest arrived in town. He had been working in India, far from where Agnes lived. She loved listening to his stories about helping the poor in the city of Calcutta.

So, when she turned 18, Agnes said goodbye to her family and started a long journey. She was determined to become a nun and help people – no matter what.

She travelled to Ireland and joined the sisters of Loreto. Once she had settled at the convent, Agnes asked the nuns to call her 'Teresa' from that day on.

A few months later, she was ready to board a ship and travel to India. The language, the colours, the food, the smells... everything was new and different for her!

Mother Teresa taught at a school for many years. But she knew there were some people who needed her more than her students: the poorest of the poor.

Mother Teresa took to the streets of Calcutta, determined to help the first person in need. She had hardly taken three steps before she stumbled upon a woman who was lying on the ground.

Soon, 12 students joined her. They called themselves the 'Missionaries of Charity' and they set out to care for all those who needed it. They chose to wear a simple sari.

Mother Teresa opened a hospital in an old Hindu temple. There was always one more bed, one more plate of rice, and one more blanket to cover whoever needed it. She knew that the smallest things could make the biggest difference.

HOSPITAL

For more than twenty years, she picked up thousands of people from the streets of India. She opened hospitals, orphanages and schools all over the world.

She received all the awards that could be given to a single person. But she only accepted them in the name of the poor.

Mother Teresa sent a beautiful message out to the world: it doesn't matter if you do big or small things in your life, as long as you do them with great love.

MOTHER TERESA

(Born 1910 • Died 1997)

c. 1925 (left)

c. 1930

Anjezë Gonxhe Bojaxhiu was of Albanian descent and born in Skopje (now the capital of North Macedonia). The Anglicised version of Anjezë (Agnes) has been used in this book. Agnes lived with her mother, father, older brother and sister. Her family followed the Roman Catholic faith, and this could be seen in their everyday life. Her family weren't rich but opened their home to people who needed help. Her mother would provide strangers with hot food and a place to rest. She taught Agnes to see God in the faces of strangers. At 12, Agnes then heard 'the call' to dedicate her life to God. Her mother thought she was too young, but the voice persisted over the next few years. Agnes was fascinated by stories of Catholic

1971

1974

missionaries, people who travelled to faraway places to help those in need. At 18, she set off to join a convent in Ireland, taking her vows as Sister Teresa. She travelled to India to teach at a school in Calcutta, where she became 'Mother Teresa'. Mother Teresa was on a train to Darjeeling when she heard the 'call within the call'. She believed God wanted her to help the poor whilst living among them. She founded the 'Missionaries of Charity' and many nuns joined her. They set up hospitals, comforted the sick and cared for the poor when no-one else did. She was awarded the Nobel Peace Prize in 1979 for her work. After she died, she was awarded a sainthood by Pope Francis in 2016. The Missionaries of Charity still continue Saint Teresa's work today.

Want to find out more about **Mother Teresa?**
Have a read of these great books:

Who Was Mother Teresa? by Jim Gigliotti and David Groff
DK Biography: Mother Teresa by Maya Gold
Mother Teresa: The Life of Mother Teresa by Paul Harrison

You can read more about the work of the Missionaries of Charity, on their website: 'The Mother Teresa of Calcutta Centre'.

Original idea of the series by Maria Isabel Sánchez Vegara, published by Alba Editorial, S.L.U.
"Little People, BIG DREAMS" and "Pequeña & Grande" are trademarks of
Alba Editorial S.L.U. and/or Beautifool Couple S.L.
First published in the UK in 2018 by Frances Lincoln Children's Books, an imprint of The Quarto Group.
1 Triptych Place, London, SE1 9SH, United Kingdom. T 020 7700 6700 www.Quarto.com
First published in Spain in 2018 under the title Pequeña & Grande Mother Teresa
by Alba Editorial, S.L.U., Baixada de Sant Miquel, 1, 08002 Barcelona, Spain. www.albaeditorial.es

A catalogue record for this book is available from the British Library.

ISBN 978-0-7112-4871-7
Set in Futura BT.

Published by Rachel Williams · Designed by Karissa Santos
Edited by Katy Flint · Production by Jenny Cundill

Printed by Replika Press Pvt. Ltd, India

3 5 7 9 8 6 4 2

Photographic acknowledgements (pages 28-29, from left to right) 1. The young Albanian born Anjez Gonxhe Bojaxhiu, with her sister Aga, in Macedonian traditional costume, c. 1925 © Vittoriano Rastelli / Corbis via Getty Images 2. Mother Teresa of Calcutta, c. 1930 © Vittoriano Rastelli / Corbis via Getty Images 3. Mother Teresa sighted on October 16, 1971 © Ron Galella / Getty Images 4. Mother Teresa with a child from the orphanage she operates in Calcutta, 1974 © Nik Wheeler / Sygma via Getty Images

MIX
Paper from responsible sources
FSC® C016779
FSC www.fsc.org

Collect the *Little People,* **BIG DREAMS**® series:

STEVE JOBS

NELSON MANDELA

ANNE FRANK

MAHATMA GANDHI

MOTHER TERESA

ALBERT EINSTEIN

BRUCE LEE

CHARLES DICKENS

MALALA YOUSAFZAI

MICHELLE OBAMA

CHARLES DARWIN

NEIL ARMSTRONG

DWAYNE JOHNSON

PELÉ

AGATHA CHRISTIE

MARTIN LUTHER KING JR.

HARRY HOUDINI

STEPHEN HAWKING

MARIE CURIE

MUHAMMAD ALI

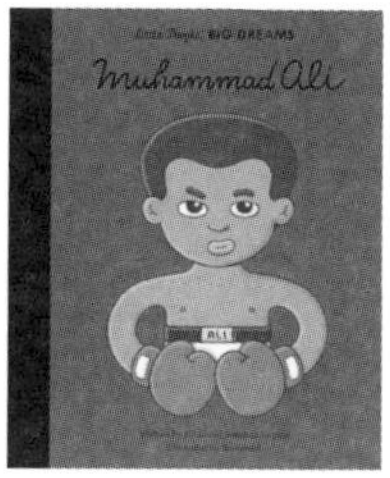

MAYA ANGELOU

Scan the QR code for free activity sheets, teachers' notes and more information about the series at www.littlepeoplebigdreams.com